THE STORY OF HOW I BECAME A VIKING

Written by Brian McFadden
Illustrated by Mario Clemente

Copyright © 2021 by Brian McFadden

All rights reserved. No part of this book may be reproduced or used in any manner without the express written permission of the author, except for the use of brief quotations in a book review. For permission requests, write to the author at the email address below.

mcfaddenbooks@outlook.com

ISBN # 978-1-7373571-0-0 (hardcover)
ISBN # 978-1-7373571-1-7 (paperback)
ISBN # 978-1-7373571-2-4 (ebook)

Dedication

For Fiona and Emmett. I love you.

*To Colleen… my editor, advisor, keeper, and all-around partner in crime.
I could not have done this without you.*

Today I'll become a Viking,
And conquer the land across the seas.

But first I'll need to build some stuff,
And ask mom to use the scissors please.

A Viking needs some protection you see,
So I'll start by making a helmet.

Mom's flowerpot is the perfect fit,
Topped with ice cream cones and red velvet!

Next I'll need some offense,
To command the kings and lords.

A blade, a brand, a cutlass,
Or a big ole shiny sword.

Too tall.   Too small.   Too heavy.

None of these will do.

This stick might do the trick, It's pretty straight and true.

It still needs something though… To give it that shiny hue.

With a touch of aluminum foil,
It's more beautiful than ever!

Now it's time to build my ship,
Which won't be an easy endeavor.

Maybe I can use Sissy's wagon,
So it won't take me forever.

Stitched together with my favorite tape,
No doubt it's something special.

I'll throw some juice over the bow,
To christen my cardboard vessel.

Here's to hoping my voyage,
Will be exciting and successful.

Wait... I almost forgot!
One more piece of the puzzle.

I need a shield for my protection,
In case I run into some muscle.

Now we part these lands,
From beneath this ancient elm.

Our eyes swell up with tears,
As the adventure overwhelms.

The voyage will be dangerous,
To conquer this unknown realm.

And as the men board the ship,
I grab ahold of the helm.

From down below you could hear the men,
The bellows, groans, and wails.

Finally we landed,
On shores unknown to man.

We were barely off the ship,
And my mates had already ran.

I had my sword and my shield,
But I didn't have a plan.

And that's when I saw him... he was huge,
Even bigger than Mom's sedan.

He was red, and fierce, and scaley,
Flying and breathing fire.

I was scared… that's for sure,
But I had all I would require.

I had strength, and guts, and valor,
And all my Viking attire!

I jumped and dashed and thrusted,
But the dragon did endure.

Only one of us could be victor,
That I knew for sure.

I was exhausted and out of steam,
But my heart was sound and pure.

I raised my sword one last time,
For victory I would secure!

At last I had won the battle,
The Dragon was done, defeated.

I took a breath and bowed my head,
My quest… finally completed.

Thank you for reading.

If you enjoyed this book, please leave a review online or write to me at: mcfaddenbooks@outlook.com

I'd love to get your feedback.

Lightning Source UK Ltd.
Milton Keynes UK
UKHW050922130821
388756UK00002B/53